For Gemk,

Whose endless supply of ideas and honest critique made this possible.

感謝 Gemk

源源不絕的靈感及誠懇的建議讓這一切成真。

An eXtraOrdinary Day

不尋常的一天

Coleen Reddy 著

安 宏 繪

薛慧儀 譯

三民書局

Ken wakes up on Friday morning.

He is not really excited. It is just another boring day at school.

He eats breakfast and reads the newspaper.

小康在星期五的早上醒來。
他並沒有覺得特別興奮，反正，不過又是待在學校，
度過無聊的一天罷了。
他一面吃早餐，一面看報紙。

He looks at his horoscope first.
He reads: "Today will be an extraordinary day.
Be extra careful when working with anything
that could explode and don't touch any balls."
He always believes what he reads.

他先看看今天自己的星座運勢如何。
報上說：「今天將會是個特別的日子，處理可能會爆炸的物品時，
要特別小心，也不要碰任何球類。」
小康對星座向來是深信不疑的。

Ken goes to school.

His first class is Science.

They are doing science experiments.

The teacher tells them to get into groups and choose a table.

Ken and his friend, Joe, choose a table and start doing the experiment.

They have to be very careful.

小康到學校上課去了。

第一堂是自然課，

他們要做科學實驗。

老師要他們分成幾個小組，各選一張實驗桌。

小康和他的朋友喬選定一張實驗桌之後，開始做實驗了。

他們一定要非常地小心。

In the middle of the experiment, Ken remembers
what he read in the newspaper.
He must be *extra* careful.
"Let me do the experiment," says Ken. "I will be extra careful."
"No," says Joe. "I'm almost finished."
But Ken tries to take the experiment away from Joe.

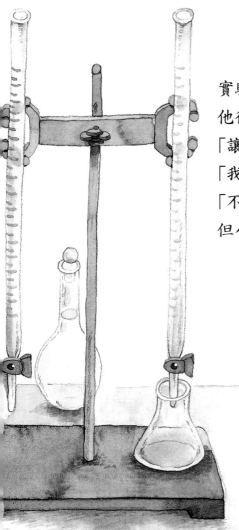

實驗做到一半，小康想起他在報紙上讀到的星座運勢。

他得特別小心才行。

「讓我來做這個實驗吧！」小康說。

「我會特別小心的。」

「不要，我已經快完成了。」喬說。

但小康還是想把喬手上的實驗瓶搶走。

9

Ken does not realize that he is shaking the experiment.
It explodes suddenly and everything falls on the floor.
"What's going on here?" yells the teacher.
Joe and Ken are not hurt, but they have to stand outside
for the rest of the class.

10

小康沒發現，其實他正在搖晃著那瓶化學液體呢！

突然間，實驗瓶爆炸了，東西也散落一地。

「發生什麼事了？」老師大喊著。

喬和小康雖然沒有受傷，但被罰整堂課都要站在教室外面。

Later, Ken has PE. He has to exercise.
Today they are playing soccer.
He loves to play soccer.

稍後，小康上體育課，必須要做運動。
今天他們要踢足球。
他最喜歡踢足球了。

13

While he is playing soccer, he remembers that
the newspaper said he *should not* touch any balls.
His friend, Joe, kicks the ball to him.
But instead of kicking the ball, he starts running away from it.
He runs into another student and falls down.

他踢足球時，想到報紙上說，他今天最好不要碰任何球類。

這時，喬把球踢給他，但小康卻沒有把球踢回去，反而連忙躲開它。

結果，他不小心撞上另一個同學而摔倒了。

"Are you okay?" asks the teacher.

"No," says Ken. "I think I broke my ankle."

The teacher takes Ken to the hospital.

「你還好嗎？」老師問。

「不……我的腳踝好像受傷了。」小康說。

於是老師把小康送到醫院去。

In the hospital, Ken has an X-ray.

His parents come over to see him.

"Ken has broken his ankle," says the doctor.

"He has to stay in bed for a week."

小康在醫院裡照了X光。

爸爸媽媽都來看他。

醫生說：「小康的腳踝骨折了，

他必須躺在床上休養一個星期。」

Ken's parents take him home.
He lies in bed.
"Why were you acting so strange today?
I heard that you also had a little accident
in Science class," says his mother.

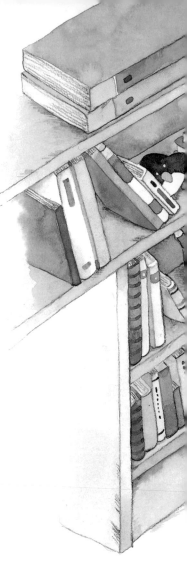

爸爸媽媽帶小康回家。
他乖乖地躺在床上。
「你今天為什麼表現得這麼奇怪？
我聽說你在自然課的時候也出了點狀況。」媽媽說。

Ken explains that he read his horoscope in the newspaper.

His mother gets the newspaper.

"You mean *this* newspaper?" asks his mother.

"Yes," answers Ken.

小康解釋說是因為他讀了報紙上的星座運勢。

媽媽把報紙拿來，「你是說這份報紙？」媽媽問。

「對呀！」小康回答。

"It's *yesterday*'s newspaper," laughs his mom.
"I hope that teaches you not to believe everything you read.
It's so silly to be superstitious. Here's today's newspaper."

「這是昨天的報紙呀！」媽媽笑著說。「我希望你經過這次教訓以後，
不會再完全相信報紙上看來的這種東西了，迷信是很愚蠢的。
來，這是今天的報紙。」

Ken feels so stupid.
What an awful experience! It does turn out to be
an *extraordinary* day but only because he is silly enough
to believe what he has read. It is all his own doing.
He can't blame his horoscope or anything else.
Now he is stuck in bed for a week.

小康覺得自己真是笨透了。
多麼慘痛的經驗呀！今天真的變成了「不尋常的一天」。
一切都是他自作自受，也不能怪星座運勢或其他什麼的。
現在他得被困在床上一個星期了。

He reads the right newspaper.
Suddenly, he notices the date on the newspaper.
It is Friday the Thirteenth!

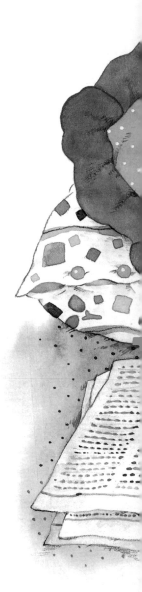

他讀起了今天的報紙。
突然間，他發現今天是十三號星期五！

"That explains everything," thinks Ken.

"It's not my fault. I couldn't help it. I was cursed."

Strangely, Ken feels better.

No, he certainly hasn't learned his lesson!

30

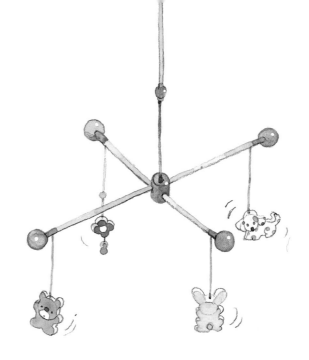

「難怪了，」小康想，「原來不是我的錯嘛，
今天是個被詛咒的日子，我也無能為力呀！」
奇怪的是，小康這麼想就覺得好多了。
唉！看來他仍然沒有得到教訓哪！

急救小常識

　　故事裡的小康因為踢足球的時候不專心,和同學撞在一起而造成了骨折。你是不是也曾經有過像小康這樣的經驗,在操場上玩耍或是上體育課時,因為一時不小心而受傷呢?來學學以下這些有用又簡單的急救小常識吧!以後如果你或是你身邊的人不小心受傷,就不會手忙腳亂、不知道該怎麼辦嘍!

現在假設你是小康的同學,而小康受了傷發生以下情況,你該…

 狀況1 快來幫忙啊!我流鼻血了!

1. 小康,快坐下,把頭向前傾,讓血流出來。不要把頭往後仰,否則血會倒流入呼吸道裡,反而會被嗆到喔!
2. 來來來,讓我幫你把脖子上的衣物(例如襯衫的領子、領帶、圍巾等等)鬆開。
3. 小康,現在要用嘴巴呼吸喔,而且要用手按住鼻子兩側、也就是鼻骨下的柔軟部位十分鐘。(如果流鼻血的原因是鼻子受到外傷,只能輕輕地按住鼻子,不可以用力壓喔!)
4. 十分鐘到了!把手鬆開讓我來看看,嗯,很好,血已經停了。(如果還不能止血,就再等十分鐘。)
5. 小康,現在你要好好休息一下,不可以摳鼻子或挖鼻孔,否則可能會再出血喔!

 　　如果出血持續超過二十分鐘,或有其他病徵(如頭部受傷等)的話,就要送醫檢查。

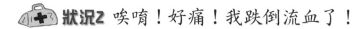 **狀況2** 唉唷！好痛！我跌倒流血了！

1. 哇，你的傷口好髒啊！來來來，讓我用消毒藥水來幫你清洗並且消毒傷口。會痛的話要忍耐一下喔！如果傷口髒髒的又不清洗的話，會引起感染的！
2. 好啦，現在只要再用乾淨的繃帶包紮就可以囉！

狀況3 上體育課時，天氣好熱好熱喔。糟糕！小康中暑了！

1. 同學們一起來幫忙把小康扶到陰涼通風的地方，讓他躺下來。
2. 小康，讓我幫你解開衣服、束帶（腰帶、領帶等等），頭部也要墊高喔。
3. 哇，你的身體好燙喔！我來用濕毛巾或酒精幫你擦擦身體，讓你的體溫馬上降下來（不過不可以低於38度喔）。
4. 來，喝杯鹽開水，補充一下身體流失的水分跟鹽分吧！

    （如果他昏迷不醒，就先別給他喝水了。注意不可以給他服用任何藥物喔！）

注意 要密切觀察中暑患者，如果有任何異常變化，就要馬上送醫。

生字表

 p. 5

horoscope [`hɔrə,skop] 名 占星術

extraordinary [,ɛkstrə`ɔrdə,nɛrɪ] 形
特別的

explode [ɪk`splod] 動 爆炸

 p. 6

experiment [ɪk`spɛrɪmənt] 名 實驗

 p. 10

yell [jɛl] 動 大聲喊叫

 p. 14

instead of 取而代之的

run into 撞到

 *p. 24*

superstitious [,supɚ`stɪʃəs] 形 迷信
的

 p. 26

awful [`ɔful] 形 極壞的

turn out （結果）變成

blame [blem] 動 責備

stuck [stʌk] 形 被困的

 p. 30

cursed [`kɝst] 形 被詛咒的

34

全新創作 英文讀本
帶給你優格（yogurt）般，青春的酸甜滋味！

Teens' Chronicles

愛閱雙語叢書

青春記事簿

大維的驚奇派對／秀寶貝，說故事／杰生的大秘密
傑克的戀愛初體驗／誰是他爸爸？
叛逆大維打工記／外星老師來上課／耶！放假了！

你我身上純真的影子，
透過一篇篇幽默風趣的故事重現，
推薦你這套青春無悔的創作系列，
讓愛玫、杰生、大維、凱爾、海倫、傑克，
帶你進入他們的世界，品味另一種學習英語的全新感受。

國家圖書館出版品預行編目資料

An eXtraOrdinary Day: 不尋常的一天 / Coleen
Reddy著; 安宏繪; 薛慧儀譯.－－初版一刷.－－
臺北市; 三民, 2003
　　面; 　公分－－(愛閱雙語叢書.二十六個妙朋
友系列) 中英對照
ISBN 957–14–3755–7　(精裝)

　　1.英國語言－讀本

523.38　　　　　　　　　　　　　92008795

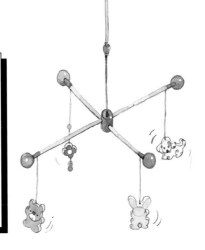

© **An eXtraOrdinary Day**
—— 不尋常的一天

著作人	Coleen Reddy
繪　圖	安　宏
譯　者	薛慧儀
發行人	劉振強
著作財產權人	三民書局股份有限公司 臺北市復興北路386號
發行所	三民書局股份有限公司 地址 / 臺北市復興北路386號 電話 / (02)25006600 郵撥 / 0009998–5
印刷所	三民書局股份有限公司
門市部	復北店 / 臺北市復興北路386號 重南店 / 臺北市重慶南路一段61號

初版一刷　2003年7月
　編　號　S 85657–1
　定　價　新臺幣壹佰捌拾元整
　行政院新聞局登記證局版臺業字第〇二〇〇號

ISBN　957–14–3755–7　(精裝)